Can I Keep it?

Licensed by The Illuminated Film Company
Based on the LITTLE PRINCESS animation series © The Illuminated Film Company 2007
Made under licence by Andersen Press Ltd., London
'Can I Keep It' Episode written by Cas Willing
© The Illuminated Film Company/Tony Ross 2007
Design and layout © Andersen Press Ltd., 2007.
Printed and bound in China by C&C Offset Printing.
10   9   8   7   6   5   4   3   2   1
British Library Cataloguing in Publication Data available.

ISBN: 978 1 84270 644 2 (Trade edition)
ISBN: 978 1 84939 696 7 (Riverside Books edition)

Can I Keep it?

Tony Ross

Andersen Press · London

The Little Princess was having a picnic in the castle grounds.

"Oooh!" she cried, as she tugged at a red packet. The packet ripped open, sending biscuits flying in every direction.

Woof! Woof!

Scruff bounded past them.

"Oh, Scruffy!" cried the Little Princess. He was heading straight for the pond.

sPLASH!

Scruff leapt into the water, drenching the pondside picnickers.

"That's naughty!" shouted the Little Princess.

Scruff clambered out and shook his fur. Puss reached for his umbrella.

"Now the food is all wet!"

The Little Princess was really cross, until she looked down at her glass. "Th-there's an animal in my drink…"

The Little Princess went straight to the Admiral.
The Admiral eyed the strange creature nervously, then pulled up his rubber ring. "There are sharks in these waters, you know."
"Is this a shark?" asked the Little Princess.
"It's difficult to know," replied the Admiral.

"A shark!" gasped the Little Princess.
"Can I keep it?"
The Admiral was in three
minds. "Yes! No! I don't know."

"That's not a shark, that's a tadpole!" cried the Maid when the Little Princess brought the glass into the laundry room. "And it belongs back where you found it!"

"But I want to keep him," argued the Little Princess. The Maid shook her head. "It'll be missing its friends." The Little Princess looked down into the glass and made a decision. "I'll be his friend."

"A tadpole is not a pet," said the Queen as she peered into the glass. "Why not?" asked the Little Princess. "Pets can be trained," answered the Queen. "Scruff and Puss are your pets."

The Little Princess
watched Scruff scratch
a flea, then looked back
at the tadpole.

"But I want this one," she begged.

"Pleeease?"

The Queen put down her knitting
and sighed. "Ask your father."

"A tadpole is a wild animal," argued the King as he flicked a tiddlywink towards the pot.

"He doesn't look very wild," said the Little Princess.

"It needs its habitat."

"I'll get him one."

At last the King agreed. "If you really look after it, then you can keep it."

The Little Princess giggled with delight, then thought for a moment. "What's a habitat?"

"A habitat is where something lives and it's full of things that make it happy," explained the Gardener. "I'll show you if you like."

"OK," smiled the Little Princess.

Inside his greenhouse, the Gardener found a glass bowl.

"We need stones, water, pond plants…"

The Little Princess watched as he added each of the things one by one.

"And not forgetting… the tadpole."

The Little Princess cheered. "Taddy!"

The Little Princess spent the whole day lying on her bed,
gazing at the tadpole.
"Aaah, Taddy," she whispered fondly.

Puss and Scruff did all their best tricks for the Little Princess, but she didn't even look up from the bowl. She was having too much fun just watching Taddy swim round and round and round. "Isn't he great?" she beamed.

The Little Princess liked making Taddy happy. In the morning, she fetched him some fresh pond water.

In the afternoon she dug up a new rock for his bowl, then rinsed it off in the sink. "I would like to take him everywhere," announced the Little Princess, as she carried the bowl into the kitchen.

The Chef shooed her
straight back out again.
"No, no, no, no, NO!"

The tadpole was the best pet the Little Princess had ever had. He was always there when she wanted to play with him and he never did anything naughty.
But one morning when she peeped into his bowl, the Little Princess got the shock of her life.

"Taddy?" asked the Little Princess.

"Ribbit," answered a creature that didn't look like Taddy at all.

"Help!" shrieked the Little Princess. "Quick!"

"A horrible animal has eaten Taddy," cried the Little Princess.

"And it's still in the bowl!"

"That is a frog," answered the Maid.

"It ate my taddypole!" sobbed the Little Princess.

The King and Queen looked at each other and chuckled.

"It didn't eat your tadpole – it *is* your tadpole!"

"Tadpoles turn into frogs," explained the Gardener.

The Little Princess was delighted. "Taddy's all grown-up,"
she beamed proudly.

"*Ribbit,*" agreed Taddy.

Suddenly the Little Princess had an idea. "I'm going to keep
my froggy for ever."

The rest of the day was spent playing with the wonderful
new pet. Puss and Scruff tried their best to join in, but they
weren't half as interesting to the Little Princess.

"Kiss Froggy," demanded the Little
Princess at bedtime.
The Queen clicked the light off.
"Goodnight!"
But it wasn't a good night at all.
"*Ribbit*," croaked Froggy.
"*RIBBIT*," echoed the frogs in the
pond outside.

Ribbit

Ribbit

Ribbit

Ribbit

Ribbit

Ribbit

Ribbit

Nobody in the castle got a wink of sleep.
The Little Princess had no choice but to pull the covers
over her head, leaving Froggy to call to his friends.

Ribbit   Ribbit

Enough was enough.

The next morning the Little Princess got up early.

"Bye bye, Froggy," she said, as she tipped him back into the castle pond. "Go and find your friends."

That night the Little Princess snuggled up in bed with Puss, just like she used to.
"*You're* a lovely quiet pet," she sighed happily.
Scruff leapt up on to the bed too. Puss tried to keep him quiet, but it was too late…

Woof!

Woof!

"Into your basket, both of you!" said the Little Princess firmly. From now on, her bedroom was *not* a place for noisy pets.